D.

I have to give the driver full credit. He was much more alert than I would have thought he might be.

He almost managed to stop.

One of the doctors in the Emergency Room asked if I had been in before. He thought I looked familiar.

I didn't answer him. I just lay there and suffered.

Three cracked ribs. Numerous contusions and abrasions, most of them coming from skidding along the concrete street. Several gashes which required stitches.

Aside from that, I was just fine. Ethel Ann couldn't wait to get me home.

MY HEART CRIES FOR YOU

FOR YOU

Bill Crider

MY HEART CRIES FOR YOU

Bill Crider

I met Ethel Ann Adams on Valentine's Day and we met cute, just like in the movies. I was in the flower department at Kroger, thinking I might buy some flowers to send to the woman who'd just ditched me two days before for a man who drove a BMW. I thought maybe she'd feel sorry for me and give me another chance. I don't know. Anyway, I was standing there looking at the roses when Ethel Ann ran into me with her grocery cart.

She didn't knock me far, not more than a foot, and I figured the bruises would go away in a week or two, so I told her not to worry about it. To forget it. I was fine.

If she'd been good-looking, it might've been a different story, but she wasn't the kind of woman I was interested in at all. She was short and chunky, about five-three and 140 pounds. Solid. She had black hair like wires — curly wires, the kind inside a sofa cushion. Those were on her head. Her mustache was black, too, but the hairs weren't curly. They were too short.

She wouldn't leave me alone, though. She acted like she'd done me irreparable harm and it was her duty to make it all right.

"Here, let me help ya," she said. She had a voice like a stevedore. "I'll pick up ya packages."

She scuttled around like a crab with Saint Vitus's Dance and picked up the cereal box and the granola bars and the Hamburger Helper, then stuffed them back on top of my basket.

"Ya okay now?" she said.

"I'm fine," I said, always the gentleman. "I'll be just fine, thanks."

"Good, good. I'm glad. Ya buying some posies for your chick?"

She really said things like that: Posies. Chick.

"No," I said. "I was thinking of sending some to my mother." My mother had been dead for ten years, but how do you say you were thinking of sending flowers to someone who'd just dumped you?

"Ya got a chick?"

"I beg your pardon?"

"Ya got a chick? A babe? A hotsie-totsie?"

She really said that. Hotsie-totsie.

"No," I said, rather coldly I'm afraid.

"A nice-looking hunk like you? All alone on the most romantic day of the year? I can't believe it."

I am rather nice-looking, I have to admit. A slight natural wave in my hair, a nice smile (thanks to extensive orthodontic work in my youth), and a trim body (thanks to a three-times-a-week jog of up to three miles).

"Ya got cute buns too."

Buns. I ask you.

"I betcha wouldn't believe I don't have a fella myself."

"Uh…"

"Yeah, I know. Hard to believe. But true." She tried to look wistful, but instead looked only dyspeptic. She had on a horrible pair of knit stretch pants that did nothing to help the effect.

"Look," she said. "Why don't you and me get together? I mean, it's a real shame, two hot numbers like us, all alone on the most important romantic day of the year."

She stood there and looked up at me with her black eyes way back in her head under the heavy ridges of her brows. The brows were black and straight, like her mustache. I had heard of the supermarket as being one of the hot places to meet dates nowadays, but this was too much. Hot numbers. I mean, give me a break.

Still, there I was. Ditched not two days before by the light of my life, who said she thought I lacked ambition and "charisma." I had told *her* that I liked selling shoes, and that you didn't need charisma to do that. She had laughed at me and said she could tell I'd never amount to anything and that she was going to start dating somebody named Chris. "He drives a BMW," she said. "Not a tacky old Subaru." I told her that Subarus had even better repair records than BMWs, but it didn't do any good.

So call it temporary insanity. Call me irresponsible. Or call me a masochist, which is probably more like it. I was punishing myself for losing somebody who liked a car better than she liked me. Anyway, for whatever reason, I looked into Ethel Ann's pitchy black eyes and said, "Why not?"

She told me her name then, and I told her mine, which is Wayne G. (for Garfield, but I never tell anyone that, not since that cat in the comic pages) Cook, and we agreed that she would come by and pick me up later at my apartment.

"I got a nice car," she said. "You'll like it. Plus I like to drive. We'll have a few drinks, tell a few jokes, see what develops."

Then she leered at me, a truly frightening sight, and icy fingers ran up and down my spine. Not the Old Black Magic kind. The kind that you get when you're reading Stephen King on a dark and stormy night, except that she was even scarier....

But I'd given my word and that was that. I finished my shopping, without buying any roses, checked out, and went home to get ready.

She arrived right on time, wearing a red skirt with a white blouse that just sort of hung on her flat chest. She had a white envelope in her hand. "Here," she said, sticking the envelope at me. "I got ya a valentine."

I hadn't gotten her one, of course. The thought never even entered my mind, and if it had I would have rejected it instantly. I took the envelope.

"Aren't ya gonna ask me in?" she said.

I opened the door a little wider and she walked through. My living room is nothing to brag about, not being much larger than most people's second bedroom, but it is at least tidy.

She walked over and sat down on the couch while I tore at the envelope. When I got it open, I pulled out the card. It was in the shape of a heart (not a real one, of course, but a valentine one, which has absolutely no relationship to the human heart that I can see) with eyes and a mouth drawn on it. The mouth was turned down in a frown, and there were tiny tears in the corners of the eyes.

I opened the card. Inside it was written in red letters, *My heart cries for you.*

"Cute, huh?" Ethel Ann said.

"Very," I said. I put the card down on my coffee table.

"So where ya wanta go?" she said. "Find a nice spot, hoist a few brewskis?"

Brewskis. Of course.

"I was thinking more along the lines of a movie," I said. The idea of what Ethel Ann might be like after a couple of "brewskis" frankly terrified me.

"Aww ri-i-i-i-ght!" she said. "There's this new one out I've been wanting to see over at the Plaza Town Eight."

"Fine," I said. "What is it?"

"It's a new one for Valentine's Day. I EAT YOUR HEART. It's about these teenagers, see, who have this Valentine's party and this maniac or something — "

"I can't wait," I said.

She was right about one thing, at least. I loved her car. It was a perfectly restored 1957 Chevrolet.

"Original factory paint," she said. "It was a bitch to find the purple, too, believe me."

"I can imagine."

"The white for the top was easy, though. I wanted to go with red, but the guy who did the work wouldn't go for it. Some people got no taste at all."

"Too right," I said.

The movie was worse than I'd thought it might be. It wasn't so much the actual movie, though the sight of entrails and brains and exploding teenage skulls didn't really do much for me. No, the worst thing was the way Ethel Ann behaved.

She belched.

I suppose that could be my fault. After all, I did ask if she wanted something to drink to go with her popcorn (two large tubs, buttered), and carbonated water does that to some people.

She didn't have to do it so often, however. I think some of it must have been deliberate.

Also, she laughed raucously every time some semi-innocent victim lost one of his or her vital body parts or got skewered with a tree limb, broken boat paddle, lug wrench, or whatever.

Everyone else cringed, gagged, or simply looked away. Not Ethel Ann. She brayed like a mule. Or is it donkeys that bray? Well, you get the idea.

And then she…there's simply no delicate way to put this, really. She…broke wind.

Loudly.

At a time when the audience sat in absolute silence as the maniac crept quietly up on yet another teenage beauty who had thoughtlessly rejected him and who in fact had laughed when he sent her a valentine.

Just as he raised his arms high, prepared to bring the jagged mop handle down into her chest as she lay sleeping on a sofa, just as the quiet in the theater had grown almost unbearable, Ethel Ann broke wind.

It was like a gunshot, but more drawn out, if you understand what I mean.

Heads turned.

Giggles began.

Ethel Ann joined in the giggles, looked at me, and pointed her finger, shaking her head sadly as if to say, "He does that all the time."

The giggles turned to laughter as I tried, without much luck, to melt through the bottom of my seat.

It was, beyond any doubt, the worst evening of my life. I can't recall ever being more repelled or disgusted. People were still giving me surreptitious glances as we left the theater. Then they would look away quickly and laugh, sometimes putting their hands over their mouths as if they didn't want me to see.

Ethel Ann wasn't bothered in the least. "That was great, huh? I don't know when I've seen so much guts on the screen."

I didn't say anything. I just wanted to get home, lock my door, and get away from her. Thank God, I would never have to see her again.

Exactly three months later, Ethel Ann Adams and I were united in what is loosely referred to as holy matrimony.

It was a lovely service, and the bride wore white. She hadn't lost any weight over the intervening months, and she looked a little like a sow stuffed into a wedding gown. Her little piggy eyes watched me from under her veil as we repeated our vows.

I managed not to throw up as I kissed her. The hairs of her little mustache pricked me under my nose.

It all came about because of her brother.

The day after Valentine's, he'd come by my apartment. It was late afternoon, and I'd just gotten in from a hard day of trying to make women's feet fit into shoes that were generally ill made and about a size too small for the feet that were being forced into them.

I wasn't in a good mood, and Ethel Ann's brother didn't cheer me up.

He stood there in my doorway wearing a lavender silk shirt and a pair of jeans so tight that you could see the outlines of certain personal portions of his anatomy. The jeans were bell bottoms, so when he told me that he was Ethel Ann's brother, I wasn't surprised. He didn't mention that he had chosen what we call these days an "alternate life-style," but then, he didn't have to. I could just tell.

His name was Raymond, and I asked him to come in. I didn't know what else to do with him.

"This is such a *sweet* little place," he said, pirouetting around to get a good look at it. "Ethel Ann said that you were charming and handsome, and she certainly didn't exaggerate. She has a tendency to do that, you know." He posed there with one hand on his hip and another in the air. "Is it all right if I sit?"

"Look," I said. "I just got in from work, and I'm not feeling too well. I'm not sure what you want, but if it's about your sister, well, I'm sorry, but I don't really think I want to see her again."

I hoped that was all it was. I hoped that Ethel Ann wasn't a recruiting service for her brother. I didn't feel like fighting him off. I really didn't.

"Oh, my dear boy," he said. "It's not at all what you think, I'm sure. Not at all. Why, you wouldn't be able to guess in a million, trillion years what I want. I'm *sure* you wouldn't."

"Why don't you tell me, then," I said.

"All right, I will, if you insist on rushing me into it. I had hoped that we might discuss the matter in a civilized manner, you know. Not rushing into it like a pair of primitives."

"I'm sorry," I said. "I'm tired, and I need my rest. If you have something to say, please say it."

"Very well. It's simple, really." He waved the hand that was in the air. "I want you to marry Ethel Ann. And then to kill her."

I just looked at him for a second or two. Then I asked him to sit down.

It was all very simple, really. I hadn't realized that Ethel Ann's father was Ronald H.

Adams, the richest man in town, an oil million-aire from one of the big booms of the Twen-ties. He was quite old now, and, according to Raymond, on his last legs.

"The old dear is going to kick off any day now," is the way Raymond put it.

As far as Raymond was concerned, that was just fine, since there was no love lost between the two of them, and that was just the problem: Raymond was cut out of the will.

"Almost, dear boy. *Almost.* Should my sweet, ingenuous sister die first, predecease me as they say in the legal offices, then the money goes to me. Not that there is much of a chance of that in the natural order of things. Ethel Ann is as healthy as a horse." He sighed. "Still, there are ways."

"Why me?" I said. "I'm just a shoe sales-man. There are professionals for that kind of thing." It wasn't that I had anything against the idea. If ever anyone deserved to go, it was Ethel Ann Adams.

"Oh, *please,*" he said. "Are you suggesting that I get some sort of *hit*man? That is so *com-mon.*"

Common. Well, he was probably right. I wondered how he and his sister got to be so different. Ethel Ann would have gone to a hitman in a minute. Less, probably.

"Besides, dear boy, don't you read the newspapers? Every single hitman in this city is a policeman working undercover. The last three people who have hired hitmen around here have wound up in prison."

"That's right," I said. "Not a nice place. You could get raped in there."

"I didn't say it didn't have its attractive side," he said. "It's just that I don't want to spend my *life* there."

"What about *my* life?"

"It would have to look like an accident, of course. There could be no question of your involvement. No hint of scandal could ever touch you."

"If that were possible, which I don't for a minute say it is, what's in it for me?"

"Why, money, of course; money, dear boy."

Of course.

It turned out that Raymond had managed to find out a good deal about me in the course of the day. As soon as he discovered that his sister had managed to find an actual *date,* he got the name and started to work. The idea had been in his head for weeks.

And I was the ideal subject, as it turned out. A man who had been recently rejected by a woman and who had a history of such rejection.

"How did you find that out?" I said.

"It was easy," he said, but he wouldn't elaborate. I didn't argue. It was true. The latest was just one of a continuing series. All of them for more or less the same reasons.

"And that's the problem we can solve," Raymond said. "You can show them that they were all wrong. You can show them that you are virtually *filled* with drive and ambition. That you can marry the richest woman in town and obtain a great deal of money in the process."

"If they can stop laughing," I said.

Raymond smiled. "People seldom laugh at rich people very long." He sounded as if he knew whereof he spoke.

"How much?" I said.

He told me. It was more than I'd ever dreamed of.

"And my share?"

"Let's say...half."

"Let's say sixty percent."

"Done," he said, and stuck out a soft pink hand.

"I don't suppose we could put this in writing," I said.

He tittered. I don't think I'd ever heard anyone titter before, but that was what he did. There's no other way to describe it. "I don't suppose we could," he said. "You'll just have to trust me, dear heart."

"I'll think about it," I said, and I did.

It took a lot of thought. I'd never even thought of killing anyone before, and it took some getting used to. On the other hand, I'd never had the chance to become a millionaire before. And, let's face it, there was never anyone on the face of the earth that I could more cheerfully kill than Ethel Ann Adams.

Raymond had given me his number. I called him back two days later. "I'll do it," I told him. "For sixty-five percent."

"Greedy, greedy," he simpered. "But all right. Sixty-five percent."

"I may need a little help."

"We'll talk about it. After the marriage."

"I've been thinking about that part. Why do I have to marry her?"

"Opportunity, of course," he said. "You'll be close to her at all times. Who knows what might come up? She might climb a ladder. Slip in the bath. And you'll be right there."

"We'll talk later," I said.

After I hung up, I called Ethel Ann and, God help me, asked her for a date.

I won't try to tell you what the marriage was like. If you have the nasty habit of imagining the bedroom scenes played out in other people's lives, then feel free to go ahead, but such events are far beyond my own poor powers of description. Suffice it to say that those scenes were as horrible as I had anticipated they might be, and in some ways even worse. I'd prefer not to think about it.

I called Raymond after a month. He said the time was "not ripe as yet, dear boy," and that his father still had a while to live. There was no rush.

I called after another month had dragged its way past, and after that I called every week. Raymond didn't seem in a great hurry.

"Remember," he said, "if anything happens too soon after the wedding, there are bound to be nasty rumors and suspicions. Caesar's wife, dear boy. Caesar's wife."

I wasn't worried about Caesar's wife. I was worried about mine. She snored like a riveter. She ate like a horse. She wallowed in the bed like a wounded rhino.

She couldn't cook, and she refused to allow me to do so, though I am fairly competent in the kitchen. "It wouldn't be right to let ya do it," she said. "I'll take care of the meals."

So we subsisted on a diet of Budget Gourmet frozen dinners, along with occasional treats such as Mrs. Paul's fish sticks and Pepperidge Farms croissant pizza.

And she was a far worse housekeeper than cook. If she used a tissue, she left it in the chair or couch. Or she tossed it aside on the rug. She never dusted, and she was too lazy even to put such dishes as we used in the dishwasher. Powder covered the washstand in the bathroom. Mildew grew rampant in the shower and in the pile of towels that began to accumulate in a corner by the shower stall.

My formerly tidy apartment into which we had moved was becoming a slum area. It was almost unrecognizable.

I tried to avoid taking her out in public. She looked far worse than when we first met. As she put it, "Now that I got ya, I can afford to let myself go."

And go she did. Up by twenty or more pounds. She quit using makeup. "Too much trouble, sweetie. Bring me another brewski."

Ah, yes, the beer. Four six-packs a day at the very least. She guzzled the stuff.

Still, her father doted on her. We visited him twice a week, every week. He was a frail old man with a pink scalp and a few strands of white hair. Hands like claws.

After every visit, I called Raymond.

"Now, now," he said. "Don't be in a rush. If you're so eager for the money, just let the old man die. Then your wife will have it all."

"I don't want her to have it. I want her out of the way. Besides, if she dies then, I'll be suspected for sure. No one knows how I can stand her anyway."

"Just smile mysteriously if they ask," he said. "And don't worry."

I did worry, though, and finally I couldn't take it anymore.   It was just after Ethel Ann threw up on the carpet — "Too many brewskis, I guess, honey" — and then passed out on the couch, leaving me to clean up the mess.

I called Raymond. "This is it," I told him. "Now, tonight."

"Wait — " he said.

I hung up the phone.

Looking at Ethel Ann there on the couch, her mouth open, the snoring rattling the windows in the apartment, I knew I could do it. Oddly enough, I'd worried about that earlier. When it came right down to it, could I actually kill another person?

The answer was yes if the person was Ethel Ann.

I didn't think much about how to do it. I concocted some wild story about rapists and killers and went to the kitchen for a knife. I didn't have a gun, or I would have used that.

I'd slit her throat, then leave. Go to a movie. Make sure I was noticed. Then come home and find her dead. I would be the grieving husband. No one would ever know.

In my current state, it even sounded logical.

I got out the knife and tested the edge with the ball of my thumb, a stupid error, since I always kept my knives sharp.

I cut a deep gash in my thumb.

Blood was running everywhere. I got a towel from under the sink and wrapped my thumb. The bitch was going to pay for this. I rarely use foul language, but that was the way I thought of her then. The bitch.

Even then I might have done it if I hadn't stepped in the vomit. I should have cleaned it up first, I know, but I forgot. In my haste, I forgot, and I put my foot right in the middle of it.

What a vile feeling that is, knowing what you've stepped in even though at the same time you're surprised. I brought one hand up and the other hand down. The sharp blade of the knife just missed the towel and sliced neatly into the palm of my hand. Neatly and fairly deeply. I hardly felt it at first.

Later, I felt it, of course.

I managed to get the towel around my hand and stop the blood. I knew the cut was bad. Somehow I didn't think the police would buy my story about the movies now. I left Ethel Ann lying there and went to the Emergency Room instead.

I said I'd been chopping lettuce, but no one really cared.

I bled a little on the seat covers of Ethel Ann's '57 Chevy. That was the only satisfaction I got.

The next time I vowed to be much more careful. And to plan better.

I waited until just the right moment, after she had drunk her daily allotment of brewskis — *beers;* after her daily allotment of beers. Then I offered to take her to the movies.

"Ya mean it? We don't hardly go out much no more."

"I mean it," I said. "NIGHTMARE ON ELM STREET V."

"Aww ri-i-i-i-ght!"

She got ready in mere moments, ready to see Freddy.

"Where's the car?" she said as we got to the street. "Has the car been stole?"

"No, no," I said. "I just had to park across the street. It's right over there." I pointed, and sure enough the car was there, right where I'd parked it. "Just a minute, before we cross," I said. "My shoelace is untied." I knew it was untied because I'd never tied it. I bent down.

My plan was simple. We lived on a fairly busy street. We were standing between two parked cars. I would wait until I heard a car coming, rise up fast, and bump Ethel Ann in her gigantic rear end.

She, in turn, would stumble in front of the oncoming car and be crushed to jelly.

It should have worked, but what happened was rather different.

Apparently, she moved. So, when I made my move, she wasn't where she should have been. That, in itself, wouldn't have been so bad.

The bad thing was that, while pretending to tie my shoe, I had actually done so. But in trying to keep an eye out for the oncoming car, tie the shoe, and judge Ethel Ann's position, I had managed to tie my shoelaces together.

I raised up, took a half step, which was all the step I could take with my shoes tied to one another, and pitched forward into the street.

I have to give the driver full credit. He was much more alert than I would have thought he might be.

He almost managed to stop.

One of the doctors in the Emergency Room asked if I had been in before. He thought I looked familiar.

I didn't answer him. I just lay there and suffered.

Three cracked ribs. Numerous contusions and abrasions, most of them coming from skidding along the concrete street. Several gashes which required stitches.

Aside from that, I was just fine. Ethel Ann couldn't wait to get me home.

"Oh, he is my ittle itsy boogums," she said. "I take care wuv itsy boogums."

Itsy boogums. Good God.

She kept me in bed and fed me Budget Gourmet, potato chips, ice cream, and brewskis — *beers*.

She kept the television set on all the time: *The Love Connection. The New Hollywood Squares. Divorce Court. The People's Court. Superior Court.* A few more weeks of convalescing, and I might have been able to pass the bar in most states. *The New Newlywed Game* was the worst. The only thing the announcer didn't ask the contestants — if indeed they should be dignified by that word — was whether they liked to grease their mates with salad oil before they "made whoopie." (I was beginning to learn where Ethel Ann picked up her expressions.) Of course, he might have asked them that on an earlier show.

"I wonder if any of 'em ever made whoopie in bed with broke ribs?" Ethel Ann said one day.   Then she leered at me. Then...frankly, I don't want to talk about it.

After more than a week, I was able to go back to work. It was a frightening experience. At odd moments I found myself wondering what Chuck Woolery was prying out of some woman about her date with the sleazoid of her choice, or whether the audience would vote for date number one, number two, or number three.

Occasionally, I would crave a brewski.

When I was getting about as scared of myself as I was of my wife, I called Raymond from work. "We've got to meet," I said.

He didn't like it, but he agreed. He was afraid of being seen with me.

We met on my lunch hour, in the third row of a movie theater, a place that showed third-run films for a dollar admission.

The theater was practically deserted, which was a good thing, since Raymond had no idea of protective coloration. He would have stood out in any crowd. It wasn't that he looked like his sister — quite the contrary. He was taller, and much thinner. Where her hair curled, his waved. Where she was coarse, he was re-fined. Except in the matter of proper dress.

It was too dark in the theater for me to tell what color his pants were, but his shirt was shocking pink. He was wearing an ascot of some dark color, and it was covered with tiny pink hearts.

My heart cries for you, I thought for some reason.

He sat down beside me. "I simply *adore* Paul Newman," he said. "He is just so *butch* with that little mustache."

So is Ethel Ann, I thought.

"But really, dear boy, we shouldn't meet like this. It's much too dangerous. What if someone should see us?"

My reputation would be ruined, I thought.

"I don't know why you're so *eager,*" he went on. "If you could only be patient, I'm sure — "

"I can't wait," I said. "I think something's happening to me. Living with your sister is doing something to me. I…I can't explain it, but I don't think I like it."

He shook his head without taking his eyes off Paul Newman, who was stalking around a pool table in full color. "I know what you mean," he said. "I went out on my own early in life for much the same reason."

"Then *why* — " I stopped and started over, realizing I had raised my voice considerably. "Then why did you do this to me?"

"To be quite frank, I thought my father would have died by now. Surely you've *seen* him?"

I admitted that I had.

"Then you know what I mean. The strength of that man amazes me."

"But couldn't I kill her now and remain a grieving widower until you get the money? Why do I have to suffer like this?"

He managed to take his eyes off the screen and look at me. "I should think that would be quite evident," he said.

"It's sure as hell not — it's surely not evident to *me.*"

He sighed theatrically. "Should she die too soon, too long before dear father's own crisis, then he would have time to change his will. Don't you see? Why the old fool might do something *drastic,* like leaving his money to the Friends of the Earth or the Save the Whales Club. Not that I don't think that whales are quite *sweet* in their own way, but really I would much prefer to see the money go to a worthier cause. Such as myself." Then he gave me the old up and under. "And you, of course."

"Of course."

"So wait. Persevere." He pronounced it with the accent on the next-to-last syllable, so that it rhymed with *ever.* "You will be rewarded in the end."

"I'll try," I said.

He looked at me kindly. "Please do, dear boy. Please do. For both our sakes."

I left the movie then. Raymond said he thought he'd stay. "That Tom Cruise is just simply *gorgeous,*" he said as I stepped into the aisle.

I looked back, and he was leaning forward in his seat. Drooling, probably.

Months went by.
Slowly.
So slowly.
Ethel Ann and I continued to visit her father. It was after one such visit that Ethel Ann said, "The old guy's lookin' better, don't ya think, hon?"

My pace faltered. She had confirmed my own suspicions. He *did* look better. Healthier, somehow.

"He's fillin' out, did ya notice? His color's better, too. He says his authur-itis" — as God is my witness, that's what she said — "is better, even. He can open and close his hands real good."

I must have shuddered then.

"What's 'a matter?" Ethel Ann said. "Is my sugar booger cold?"

Sugar booger. Holy shi — I mean, good grief.

It was a few weeks later that I noticed that I was eager to get home after work in time for *Wheel of Fortune*.

"That Vanna's such a doll," Ethel Ann was fond of saying. "If we ever have a kid" — she leered hopefully — "a girl kid, let's name her Vanna."

"I...uh...it's a lovely name," I said.

"And that Pat Sajak? A doll. Just a doll. Lucky for you ya got me when ya did. I could really go for a guy like that."

"Be quiet," I said. "You made me miss what letter that idiot asked for."

"It was an *m,*" she said. "I thought it was a pretty good guess, myself."

"Hush," I said. "I'll miss the next one, too."

And it wasn't long after that when I realized that I was getting used to the filthy apartment. I tossed my towel on the floor right by Ethel Ann's, though I still used one more often than she did.

"After all, I hardly done a thing today," she said. "Why bathe?"

Why, indeed?

The dirty dishes piled up, the Budget Gourmet containers accumulated in the trash can, and there was actual grit on the kitchen floor. I saw roaches creeping and scuttling across the cabinets.

And at work I wondered: Who will sit in
the center square on *New Hollywood Squares*
today? And I wondered: Why didn't that fool
take door number three yesterday? Anybody
would have taken door number three. And I
wondered: How could that nincompoop not
have written down his answer in the form of
a question? Does he have a death wish?

Worst of all was the time I thought, Gee, I
wish I had me a brewski. It made my palms
sweat, and my hands slipped on the smooth
brown leather of the shoe I was trying to force
onto the foot of a woman who obviously
should have asked for a much larger size.

"What's the matter with you, fella?" she
said. "Trying to feel me up?"

"You wish," I said. It slipped out. Hon-
estly.

"What did you say, buster?"

"I...uh...said this *shoe* ish sized wrong.
I'm shorry."

She looked at me with a great deal of sus-
picion, but she let it pass. She didn't buy any
shoes, though.

I knew then that it couldn't go on any
longer. I didn't care if Mr. Adams left his

considerable fortune to Morris the Cat or the Liberace Museum.   Something terrible was happening to me, and the longer I lived with Ethel Ann, the worse it got.   I was crazy to have gone along with Raymond in the first place.   For my own sanity, Ethel Ann had to go.   And she had to go soon.

I didn't say anything about it to Raymond. There was no need for him to know, and I was sure he would have objected. He would have had good reason. Only two days before, Mr. Adams had gotten so much better that he had asked the doctor for an exercise program.

There was no doubt in my mind that he would live to be a hundred.

This time I made sure that nothing could go wrong.   I planned everything carefully, even went over it in a practice run of sorts. This time was for keeps.

I waited until the perfect night — dark, cloudy, a little drizzle. I asked Ethel Ann if she'd like to take a drive.

"Gee, I don't know, hon. On *Lifestyles of the Rich and Famous* tonight, Robin Leach is gonna give us a tour of one of Wayne Newton's places."

"No kidding? Well — No. *No.* We really ought to get out more. All we do is watch the tube — the television set. A little drive is what we need. And you know?" I smiled at her in what I hoped was a provocative manner. "A drive in the cool night air just might give me some hot ideas."

She jumped off the couch. Well, actually, she more or less rolled off. At her size and weight, which must have been nearing 190 by then, jumping was more or less out of the question. "Why didn't ya say so the first time, sport? Lemme get some shoes on."

She did, and we left.

"Let me drive," I said. "I like to drive the Chevy."

"Fine by me, kiddo. That way I can snuggle-bunny on you."

Snuggle-bunny. Give me strength.

We drove around town for a while, nowhere in particular, listening to the radio. Ethel Ann had put a really good stereo in the old car, and a good set of speakers. Unfortunately, she usually insisted on playing her Slim Whitman tapes, but tonight she had forgotten them in her haste to get out to the car and make snuggle-bunnies.

Then I headed out toward Mount Granton.

She caught on fast. "I know where y're goin', big boy," she said. "Thinkin' about makin' a little time, huh?" She wormed her way even closer to me. "Well, I'll tell ya, ya got a good chance."

I held my gorge down and kept driving. Mount Granton was a popular spot for parking and engaging in sexual activity. It had quite a good view of the city, actually, and at night the lights could look quite attractive if you were in the right mood. Of course, on such a rainy night as this, there wouldn't be many couples there. The view was terrible, it was cold, and these days most people simply preferred to stay at home and do it in bed.

Or at least, so I hoped.

Near the top, there was a small turnout. As we neared it, I said, "Gosh, honey, I think there's something wrong with one of our tires."

There was, too. I'd let a great deal of the air out of it when I came home that afternoon. Not enough to be really bothersome, but enough to be noticeable if someone called your attention to it.

"It's in the back on my side, I think," I said.

She raised her head as if that would help her to sense it. "Ya may be right," she said. "It's kinda bumping."

And that was true, too, not that I'd planned it. Just a little luck for a change. Things were at last about to go my way.

It was about time, after all.

"Why don't I pull up here," I said. "I can get out and check it." I gave a delicate cough. "I wish I didn't feel like I was coming down with a cold."

"If ya are, ya better not get your tootsies wet. I'll check it out for ya."

"How very thoughtful," I said.

I pulled into the turnout very carefully, just the way I had practiced it. Just the right angle. I stopped the car. Not a single automobile had passed us on the way up.

Goodbye, Ethel Ann, I thought.

Or maybe I said it aloud. She laughed. "I'll be right back, ya big jerk."

That's what *you* think, my dear.

I could visualize myself talking to the police officer, tears of sorrow welling in my eyes. "It...it was terrible, officer. I suppose my foot

slipped off the brake — God knows how! —
just as she was crossing behind the car. It
struck her, and the railing — the railing there
is so low! There was nothing I could do to
save her! Oh, my sweet darling!"

And at that point I would break down in
body-shaking sobs, the drizzle in the night air
blending with the tears that flowed down my
innocent cheeks.

As a plan, it was perfect.

The execution of it, however, was flawed.

In order to be sure that I struck her hard
enough, I was going to have to do a bit more
than let the car roll backward. I was going to
have to put it into reverse and give her a good,
solid bump.

Even at that, I might have succeeded had
I not been overly eager. I should have waited
until she got right in the middle, but I didn't.
I let her take one step behind the car, and
shifted gears. She saw the backup lights and
stepped back to the side.

I got my foot off the gas and back on the
brake, but the surface was extremely slick,
possibly oily. The guardrail was no help at all.

I remember hearing it splinter, my foot still
frozen to the brake. I remember the rear end

of the car tilting out over the ledge and the hood rearing up in the air.

I remember looking out the window at Ethel Ann's horror-stricken face.

And that's all I remembered for quite some time.

When I woke up in the hospital, all I could think of was how cold it seemed and how thirsty I felt.

I tried to move, I think, but that proved to be impossible. I was encased in casts and had one leg suspended in some sort of medieval torture device. The pain was excruciating.

I fainted.

When I came out of it again, I felt better, though not much. There was a nurse in my room. I tried to say something to her, but I found I couldn't talk. It was as if my tongue had swollen until it filled my entire mouth. So I just lay there. Then I went to sleep.

I woke up more and more often, and the nurses and doctors seemed to be encouraged by my progress. Ethel Ann was there most of the time. I tried not to look at her.

One day she asked me how I was feeling. I surprised myself by being able to answer. After that we talked a little.

I had been in the hospital for three weeks. In another three I might be able to go home, if I behaved myself and was a good little boy.

"My itsy boogums will be good," she said. "I will take care wuv my itsy boogums."

It hardly bothered me.

I got better and was able to watch the tube. I watched all the game shows that came on, which meant that I got to see a few I'd missed because of work, like *The Price is Right*. I also got to see Donahue, and by the time I was ready to go home I knew I'd miss him when I had to go back to work, even if he was a little bit wimpy.

Then one day Ethel Ann came in crying. "What's the matter?" I said. "Have you talked to the doctor? He didn't say anything that he told you not to tell me, did he?"

And then an even more terrible thought struck me. "Ethel Ann — your father. He's not...he didn't..."

She looked at me and I could see that she wasn't sad at all. She was actually smiling, but the tears were running down her face and she was sobbing. "It's Daddy," she said. "It's Daddy."

I was out of traction by then, almost ready to go home. Just the casts here and there. One arm (the left) and one leg (the right), plus wrappings around my ribs (broken again, five this time). I sort of fell back in the bed in a collapse.

The old man was dead.

She was trying to keep a good face on things, but the tears gave it all away. He was dead, and that was that. If I killed Ethel Ann now, everyone would suspect me.

I tried to do the right thing. "I...I'm sorry," I said.

Ethel Ann wiped the back of her hand across her eyes and pulled at her nose with her fingers. "Don't be sorry," she said. "It's just that I'm so happy."

"Happy?" I said.

"That Daddy's doing so well."

"Uh...well?"

"Yeah. I was gonna surprise ya when ya got out of the hospital. He's been just gettin' better and better ever' day. Strong as an ox. I just found out he's gonna run in the Won-Ton Marathon."

"He's...going to run...in a marathon?"

She rubbed her face, which made it look redder than ever. "Ain't it great? It's like, you know, a miracle. The doctor says he may live another hundred years."

Something came over me. I don't know what. I just knew that I had to do it then, no matter what. I came off the bed at her.

At least that's what I tried to do. I remember the leg with the cast hitting the floor and skidding. I remember the sound of the bedpan clattering across the floor. I remember falling.

I remember Ethel Ann telling the doctor, "He was so excited about my news that he tried to get up. I didn't know it would make him do that, honest I didn't."

And the doctor saying, "It's not your fault; don't worry."

So I had to stay in the hospital for a while longer, and watch a bit more television. I got real good at *The Wheel of Fortune*. Did a little more study for the bar exam with Judge Wapner. Ate hospital food.

Eventually I got to go back to the apartment. What it looked like after more than a month of Ethel Ann's care and hers alone, I can hardly tell you. There were piles of dirty clothes on the couch. The roaches had moved to the coffee table. There were coffee cups on top of the TV set. With cold coffee in them. Some of them had mold growing on the top of the coffee. It was yellowish, with green around the edges.

Ethel Ann shoved the dirty clothes from the couch to the floor and installed me on the hide-a-bed. "This'll be fun," she said. "We can watch a lotta TV."

And we did. And we drank brewskis. And we ate Budget Gourmet. Drank Diet Pepsi. Ate ice cream. And watched TV.

Finally all the casts were gone. I could walk almost as well as I had before. I could have worked at the shoe store, but I had long since been replaced. They were very sorry, but that was all.

One day when Ethel Ann was out for more junk food, I called Raymond. I named the movie theater where we'd met before and gave him a time. I told Ethel Ann that I had to get out for exercise and some fresh air.

"Is it the Glade I've been spraying? I could change brands."

I assured her that the house smelled fine. It smelled like a gymnasium built in a pine forest, but I didn't say that part.

"What, then? Exercise? That stuff'll kill ya."

I assured her that I wouldn't be long, and I went.

Raymond showed up on time. He was a little bit put out that the movie was CRIMES OF THE HEART. *"Hon*estly, Diane Keaton should never have let herself go like that, even to get the part. And Jessica Lange? My dear, she should at least have used a little makeup."

I wasn't interested in his criticisms of the movie. I had Siskel and Ebert for that. And Harris and Reed. I had another thing entirely on my mind. I told him.

"Yes, it's really too bad that it turned out this way," he said. "It seemed like such a good idea at the time," he said.

"That's all you've got to say?"

"I'm sorry, dear boy. What else *can* I say?"

"How could you ever have come up with such a harebrained scheme in the first place?" I said.

"I've often wondered. I don't think I ever took it really seriously. I *did* hope to get the money, but I suppose that will never happen, not now. *C'est la vie.*"

"*C'est la vie?*"

"French, dear boy. It means — "

"I know what it means," I said. "What about me?"

"You?"

"Me. The man married to your sister. What about me?"

"Well," he said, "there's always divorce."

"Divorce," I said.

"I suppose she'd never agree to it. Well, one has to make the best of things."

I looked at him. It was dark, but I think he was laughing at me, quietly.

So I killed him.

It was quite easy, much easier than all my attempts with Ethel Ann. I simply stepped across him to the aisle, then looked back and bent down.

"That's a lovely ascot," I said.

He simpered. "Thank you. It's pure silk. You don't think the color is a trifle…much?"

"Chartreuse? Don't be silly." I reached out my fingers to touch it.

And before he knew it, I had it off, twisted around his neck, and tight, so tight that he

could only gargle. On the screen, Sissy
Spacek was trying to hang herself, and the two
or three other customers were more interested
in her troubles than in Raymond's. I sat in the
seat behind him and slowly strangled the life
out of him. Then I left him there.

When I got back to the apartment, Ethel
Ann met me at the door. She had an envelope
in her hand. "Do ya know what day this is?"
she said.

"No," I said. "I don't believe I do."

"That's what happens when ya spend all ya
time inside. I guess gettin' out is good for ya
sometimes. Anyhow, it's a special day for us."
She handed me the envelope.

Then I knew, of course. How sentimental.
I hadn't really suspected her of being so sentimental.

She walked toward the kitchen. "I'll get us
some brewskis to help us celebrate," she said.
"Open it up. It's special."

I opened the envelope, though I already
suspected what I would find inside. I was
right. A duplicate of the valentine she'd given
me exactly one year before.

I looked at the face on the heart, the downturned mouth, the tears.

I looked up at the apartment, the filth, the roaches, the coffee cups, the clothes in piles, the plates full of crusts and crumbs.

I opened the card.

My heart cries for you.

I saw Ethel Ann heading toward me with the brewskis.

And cries, I thought.

And cries.

BILL CRIDER is the author of ten mystery novels. His series characters include Sheriff Dan Rhodes, college English professor Carl Burns, and private eye Truman Smith. His nonseries novels to date are BLOOD MARKS and THE TEXAS CAPITOL MURDERS. He also writes Westerns and has published several horror novels under the name "Jack MacLane." He and his wife, Judy, live in Alvin, Texas, where he is the chairman of the English Department at Alvin Community College.

SHORT STORY PAPERBACKS

1) LOSERS' NIGHT *Poul Anderson*
2) A CASE OF PAINTER'S EAR *John Brunner*
3) XOLOTL *Robert Sheckley*
4) ALL THE CLOCKS ARE MELTING *Bruce Boston*
5) BLOSSOMS *Kim Antieau*
6) ECCE HOMINID *Esther M. Friesner*
7) A CASE OF MISTAKEN IDENTITY *L. Timmel Duchamp*
8) THE CUTTER *Edward Bryant*
9) THE GIRL WHO FELL INTO THE SKY *Kate Wilhelm*
10) YOURS TRULY, JACK THE RIPPER *Robert Bloch*
11) THE STEEL VALENTINE *Joe R. Lansdale*
12) THE QUICKENING *Michael Bishop*
13) THE DOORS OF HIS FACE,
      THE LAMPS OF HIS MOUTH *Roger Zelazny*
14) MORE THAN THE SUM OF HIS PARTS *Joe Haldeman*
15) NO WAY STREET *Bruce Clemence*
16) THE SPIDER GLASS *Chelsea Quinn Yarbro*
17) UNCLE DOBBIN'S PARROT FAIR *Charles de Lint*
18) DINOSAURS *Walter Jon Williams*
19) LISTENING TO BRAHMS *Suzy McKee Charnas*
20) BLACK AIR *Kim Stanley Robinson*
21) THE DARK COUNTRY *Dennis Etchison*
22) JOURNEY TO THE GOAT STAR *Brian W. Aldiss*
23) PIECEWORK *David Brin*
24) I REMEMBER, I REMEMBER... *Mary Caraker*
25) SEDALIA *David J. Schow*
26) SLUMMING IN VOODOOLAND *Brian Stableford*
27) THE SWORD AND THE STONE *Jane Yolen*
28) THE WAR OF THE ROSES *Karen Joy Fowler*
29) THE CAT WITH THE TULIP FACE *A. R. Morlan*
30) TWILIGHT TIME *Lewis Shiner*

$1.95 Each; 30 Books...$55.00; 60 Books...$100.00
DON'T MISS A BOOK! SUBSCRIBE NOW!
PULPHOUSE PUBLISHING, INC.
Box 1227, Eugene, OR 97440

SHORT STORY PAPERBACKS

31) WHERE THE SUMMER ENDS   *Karl Edward Wagner*
32) INTO GOLD   *Tanith Lee*
33) DAISY, IN THE SUN   *Connie Willis*
34) INUIT   *M. Shayne Bell*
35) THE SHADE OF LO MAN GONG   *William F. Wu*
36) BUCKETS   *F. Paul Wilson*
37) THE PEAR-SHAPED MAN   *George R. R. Martin*
38) THE EVENING AND THE MORNING
     AND THE NIGHT   *Octavia E. Butler*
39) THE PEACEMAKER   *Gardner Dozois*
40) THE HERO AS WERWOLF   *Gene Wolfe*
41) THE BINGO MASTER   *Joyce Carol Oates*
42) SCHRÖDINGER'S KITTEN   *George Alec Effinger*
43) SISTERS   *Greg Bear*
44) THE GHOSTS OF TIVOLI   *Nancy Holder*
45) DR. PAK'S PRESCHOOL   *David Brin*
46) TIGHT LITTLE STITCHES
     IN A DEAD MAN'S BACK   *Joe R. Lansdale*
47) FIDDLING FOR WATERBUFFALOES   *S. P. Somtow*
48) RACHEL IN LOVE   *Pat Murphy*
49) UNACCOMPANIED SONATA   *Orson Scott Card*
50) NINE LIVES   *Ursula K. Le Guin*
51) THE SKULL OF THE MARQUIS DE SADE   *Robert Bloch*
52) MERLIN DREAMS IN
     THE MONDREAM WOOD   *Charles de Lint*
53) THE PRICE OF ORANGES   *Nancy Kress*
54) IF THIS IS WINNETKA,
     YOU MUST BE JUDY   *F. M. Busby*
55) MY BROTHER'S KEEPER   *Pat Cadigan*
56) THE THERMALS OF AUGUST   *Edward Bryant*
57) PAPER DRAGONS   *James P. Blaylock*
58) KIRINYAGA   *Mike Resnick*
59) CANDLES ON THE POND   *Sue Ellen Sloca*
60) SHAUNESSY FONG   *William F. Wu*
